THE
KING'S STILTS

WRITTEN AND ILLUSTRATED

by

Dr. Seuss

RANDOM HOUSE • NEW YORK

This title was originally cataloged by the Library of Congress as follows:
Seuss, Dr. The King's stilts; written and illus. by Dr. Seuss. Random House 1939 unp. illus.
The King wears his stilts every day after work—until they are stolen by a wicked man.
Then the Nizzards invade the country until Eric, his page boy, finally recovers the stilts and the country is saved.
1. Picture books for children   2. Wit and humor—Fiction. I. Title   E   PZ7.G272Ki   39-25149
ISBN: 0-394-80082-6 (trade) ; 0-394-90082-0 (lib. bdg.)

Manufactured in the United States of America

FOR
ALISON MARGARET BUDD
AND
DEIRDRE CLODAGH BUDD

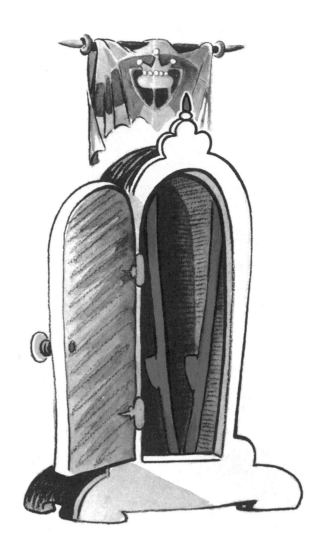

$\mathcal{N}$aturally, the King *never* wore his stilts during business hours. When King Birtram worked, he really WORKED, and his stilts stood forgotten in the tall stilt closet in the castle's front hallway.

There was so much work to be done in the Kingdom of Binn, that King Birtram had to get up every morning at five. Long before the townsfolk and the farmers were awake, the King was splashing away in his bath. It was right there, in fact, that his day's work began. With his left hand he could bathe with his royal bath brush, but his right hand he always had to keep dry for signing the important papers of state.

Eric, his page boy, brought in these papers on a big silver tray. He stood at attention at the foot of the tub, while old Lord Droon took the papers one by one and held them over the water for His Majesty to sign.

"Sign here . . . sign there," old Droon would say, "and hurry, Sire, hurry. There are hundreds more to come."

It was just the same at breakfast. The King cut and buttered his toast with only his left hand. With his right, he kept signing royal orders and commands.

By seven every morning the King had always finished more business than most kings do in a month. He *had* to get all this done before seven, for that was the hour when his Big Work commenced —the most difficult and important work in the whole Kingdom of Binn.

This was the work of caring for the mighty Dike Trees that protected the people of Binn from the sea. The sea pushed against the kingdom on three sides. The kingdom was a low one; the sea was a high one; and only the Dike Trees kept the sea from pouring in. They grew so close together in a row along the shore, that they held back the water with their heavy, knotted roots.

But to keep these trees strong and sturdy was not an easy task.

They were more spicy than pine trees, and their roots were very tasty to a certain sort of bird. This was a kind of giant blackbird with a sharp and pointed beak. Nizzards, they were called by the people of Binn. These Nizzards were always flying about over the Dike Trees, waiting for a chance to swoop down and peck. If nobody stopped them, the roots would soon give way. Then the sea would pour in with a terrible roar, and every last soul in the kingdom would drown.

But King Birtram did not permit this to happen.

He had gathered together in his kingdom the largest and the smartest cats in all the world, and had trained them to chase the Nizzards away. These cats were called Patrol Cats and wore badges that said "P. C."

"Everything in Binn," said King Birtram, "depends on our Patrol Cats. They are more important than our army, our navy, and our fire department too, for they keep the Nizzards away from the Dike Trees, and the Dike Trees keep the ocean back out of our land."

A thousand cats in all! They divided up the work: five hundred guarded the kingdom by day; the other five hundred kept watch through the night.

At seven every morning, came the Changing of the Cat Guard. At the sound of a trumpet, the King left his breakfast and mounted his horse for the daily review. Fresh, brisk and well-fed, the five hundred Day Cats marched past him toward the Dike Trees to take up their watch.

At the same time, the Night Cats, muddy, tired and hungry, headed home to their kennels for their twelve hours' rest.

There was rest for the cats. There was none for the King. It took every minute of his morning to see that they were given the very best of care. The huts that they slept in must be kept clean and tidy. Each cat must be brushed and his whiskers trimmed just so.

The Cat Kitchen was even bigger and grander than the King's, and the cooks who did the cooking were the chief cooks in the land.

"Your Majesty," the Chief-in-charge-of-Fish would always say, "tell us that you think the food we feed our cats is perfect." And the King would look over the huge wet baskets of fish, choosing only the finest and the freshest to serve to his Patrol Cats.

So went the morning. Then all afternoon, both in winter and summer, the King made his rounds by the edge of the sea. Every root of every Dike Tree he inspected every day.

But finally, at five o'clock, the great task was finished!

Then the King smiled. "A hard day," he'd say, "full of nizzardly worries. A long day," he'd say. *"Now it's time for some fun!"*

This was the moment King Birtram lived for. When he worked, he really worked . . . but when he played, he really PLAYED!

"Quick, Eric!" he'd shout. "Quick, Eric! The stilts!"

Down the slope from the Dike Trees, away from all troubles, the King and Eric would race like two boys—straight to the tall stilt closet in the castle's front hallway.

Out came the stilts! Up leapt the king!

High in the air, his royal robes streaming, he'd race through the marble halls . . . out across the terrace . . . up and down the garden stairs. Black-spotted coach dogs barked and romped beside him, nipping at the heels of his flashing red stilts.

The townsfolk looked on from the walls and just loved it. "A grown-up King on stilts," they'd say, "*does* look rather strange. But it's hard work being King, and he does his work well. If he wants to have a bit of fun . . . sure! . . . let him have it!"

But there was one man in Binn who didn't like fun. He didn't like games. He didn't like laughing. This man was a scowler. This man was Lord Droon. "Laughing spoils the shape of the face," he declared. "The lines at the corners of the mouth should go *down*."

Every afternoon when the Stilt Hour drew near, Lord Droon would slink away to his room in the northwest tower and sulk. "*Such carryings on!*" he would mutter in disgust, as he spied on the King from his window. "*Look at his crown!* Bouncing up and down on the side of his head! *Look at his beard!* Flapping in the wind! *Look at him laughing!* Right out in broad daylight in front of the townsfolk! . . . I must do something about this."

And one day he did.

One Wednesday, just before supper, when he thought the King was out, Lord Droon tiptoed down to the front hall. The guards, at their posts, were dozing. Without the smallest sound on the hard stone floor, Droon crept to the stilt closet, pulled back the ancient door and reached in. . . .

It took only a second. He had the King's stilts! He unbuttoned the top of his long robe and shoved them down inside. Then he sneaked past the guards again and slipped through the door.

Down the steep slanting stairway, Lord Droon marched with the stilts. Down to the furnace to burn them! "This is the end of the King's foolish stilt-walking," he mumbled to himself.

Then suddenly, from around the bend of the stairs below, came the sound of happy whistling. The King!

Lord Droon stopped still, almost frozen with fright. He tugged and pulled at his long flowing gown, struggling to cover the stilts. But he couldn't. The ends were too long and stuck out.

"Droon, Droon!" gasped Lord Droon, "you'll be caught!" He turned and fled back up the stairway.

Nearer and nearer came the King, but Droon couldn't climb any faster. The stilts clattered; they banged and spanked against his knees.

He looked up and saw a window. Stepping up to it quickly, he poked his head out. He looked down into an alley.

A small boy was passing.

It was Eric, the page boy.

"Psst . . . You . . . *You* . . ." Lord Droon hissed in a hoarse, nervous whisper.

Eric looked up, astonished. "Yes, sir?" He bowed politely.

"Take these stilts," commanded Lord Droon. "Take them away . . . bury them . . . deep, where no one can ever find them . . . bury them up by the sea by the Dike Trees." Lord Droon flung the stilts from the window.

The *King's stilts!* Bury them? Eric didn't know what to think. "It will spoil all His Majesty's fun!" he stammered.

"You're impudent," said Lord Droon harshly. "I said bury those stilts. What's more, young man, don't you ever come back or I'll have you locked up. I'll have no impudent boy around this castle."

"But I'm the King's own page boy!" gasped Eric, hardly able to understand this dreadful command.

"You WERE the King's own page boy!" snapped Lord Droon. He pulled in his head and slammed down the window.

Never before had Eric been so puzzled. Never in his life had he felt so sad. But there was nothing to do but obey the command. He picked up the stilts and walked straight toward the road that led to the sea.

It was the hour that the townsfolk were all having supper. Nobody saw him dig the deep hole. Nobody saw him bury the stilts.

At five the next afternoon, the halls of the castle echoed the King's mournful shouts. "Droon! . . . Droon! . . . They're gone! *They're gone!*" The King stood groping in the empty stilt closet, hopelessly searching for what wasn't there.

Lord Droon chuckled to himself. He had expected this to happen and was ready with his lie. "It was the townsfolk who did it," he said, peering into the stilt closet and pretending to be greatly shocked. "I have seen them every day, plotting behind the castle walls. 'A King,' they say, 'should behave like a King, and sit with pomp and dignity upon his royal throne. A King,' they say, 'should never walk on stilts!' It's too bad, Your Majesty, but you must try to do without them."

King Birtram answered with a heartbroken sigh. "Well . . . I'll *try* to do without them."

But he couldn't.

Day after day he grew sadder and sadder. For long hours he'd just sit, idly drumming with his fingers on the arms of his throne.

He couldn't keep his mind on his work. His commands to the Patrol Cats sounded feeble and faint. The cats seemed to know it and wouldn't obey.

Day by day they grew lazier and lazier. Uncombed and unbrushed, they slept most of the day and grew fat. No one bothered to put their P. C. badges on them, for as chasers of Nizzards they weren't worth a thing.

Day by day the Nizzards grew bolder and bolder. They cackled and fluttered over the Dike Trees. They flew down, and almost seemed to sneer at the lazy, sleeping cats.

The townsfolk began to feel frightened. Housewives couldn't keep their minds on their housework. They heard Nizzards flapping over their rooftops and poked their heads out for a look. "If the cats don't keep those Nizzards away from our Dike Trees," they asked one another, "what will keep the ocean back out of our land?"

Bootmakers couldn't keep their minds on their boots. Goldsmiths couldn't keep their minds on their gold.

Cart drivers couldn't keep their minds on where they were going. They'd stop their carts on the road and talk in low, excited whispers.

"Look at those Nizzards! . . . Where *are* the cats?"

"I'll tell you where the cats are . . . everywhere they shouldn't be and mostly fast asleep."

"Something must be wrong with the King."

"Yes, something's certainly wrong with the King!"

Only Eric, the page boy, knew what was wrong. Night after night he tossed in his bed, thinking of the stilts lying deep underground. Finally, one night he could stand it no longer. Droon or no Droon, he would go to the King!

At dawn the next day, he leapt out of bed and made straight for the castle. Breathless and panting, he raced through the royal gates and up the broad stairs.

The King was strolling sadly on the terrace, with Lord Droon and two guards.

Eric rushed up. He *must* tell the King. Droon or no Droon, he was going to tell!

But Lord Droon saw him coming and stepped quickly forward. "Impudent boy, what are *you* doing here?"

Before Eric could answer and push past him to the King, Lord Droon had grabbed him. He looked at Eric sharply and suddenly the corners of his mouth turned up in a grin. A shrewd, evil grin. "Your face . . . !" he said. *"What's wrong with your face?"*

"My face . . . ?" said Eric. He rubbed his hand over his forehead. It was merely hot and moist from running. "Nothing at all is wrong with my face."

"It's red," said Lord Droon, with the sly look he always had when he lied. "It's awfully, awfully RED. MEASLES!" he shouted. "Ho, guards . . . take him away! Lock him up!

"I haven't measles any more than you have," shouted Eric. "It's a trick—a nasty, Droonish trick! Let me talk to the King!"

But they dragged poor Eric, fighting and kicking, away from the King and down the castle stairs.

Five minutes later Eric found himself locked up in an old deserted house on the edge of the town.

From his second story window he could see the two guards, spears crossed, just below him, barring the door. Through the roof he could hear the noises of the Nizzards. Their beaks were hard as iron and scratched through the air.

Eric shuddered. There *must* be a way to escape. Round and round the room he paced, thinking and thinking.

He went to the window and looked down again. Then he whistled softly. He had an idea.

Very quickly, Eric slipped off his belt. He pushed the end through the buckle and made a lasso. Then he leaned from the window and aimed for the spear points. He dropped the loop. It caught! He jerked the belt tight and tied a quick knot.

"Look, guards, look!" shouted Eric, as he jumped up on the window sill. "Your spears are tied together!"

If the guards had dropped their spears, they could have caught him in a second. But they didn't. They just yelled at each other, and yanked and tugged, stupidly trying to pull the spears apart.

By the time they finally had them untied, Eric had sprung to the tree outside his window, slid down the trunk, and quietly escaped.

Eric ran.

Through backyards and alleyways to escape the angry guards! The streets were deserted. No people at all! They were all at home, trembling, with their window shades pulled down.

The air was full of the chittering and the chattering of Nizzards. They were cutting through the clouds like flying black knives . . . flying nearer . . . flying lower . . . down to earth to eat the Dike Tree roots . . . soon to let the sea pour in.

Eric ran.

He turned a corner. He stopped and stared with horror! Flowing gently toward him down the sloping alley came a little trickling stream. "Water!" he whispered hoarsely. He dipped in his finger. It tasted of salt. "*Sea* water!" One Dike Tree must already have been eaten clean through!

"Not a second to lose," gasped Eric. "I must dig up the stilts."

Up the hill to the Dike Trees where the King's stilts lay buried
. . . right into the very thick of the Nizzards! They flapped and
screeched about him. They hissed as he dug.

"G-r-ritch . . . G-r-ritch!" snarled the Nizzards.

"*G-r-ritch* to *you!*" snapped back Eric, furiously pelting them with
fistsful of mud.

The harder they fought him, the faster he dug. His fingers
touched the stilts at last. He pulled them from the ground.

Stilts bouncing on his shoulder, again Eric ran. The road to the
castle took him back through the town. The streets were still
deserted.

Close by the door of an old tailor shop, Eric stopped for an instant to rest. The stilts had begun to hurt his shoulder. "Those two stupid guards," he thought. "I wonder where *they* are."

He found out all too soon. From around the corner, at his very elbow, suddenly bellowed, the angry voice of old Lord Droon. "You *guards!* Guards indeed! To let a little pipsqueak of a boy tie up your spears! *Dunderheads!* Search every street . . . search every house. . ."

Eric heard the clatter of their heavy hobnail boots. No time to run! Nowhere to hide! *Wait* . . . ! Those clothes in the tailor shop . . . ! Eric ducked inside.

An instant later, Lord Droon and the guards appeared around the corner. "Search that tailor shop first," commanded Lord Droon.

But just as he said this, from out of the shop strode a strange tall man. There was something very odd about the hang of his robe. His hat was pulled down, far over his eyes.

"Those eyes . . ." muttered Droon. "Have I seen them before?" He stepped in front of the tall man, blocking his path.

The tall man's mouth went suddenly dry. "Are you . . . are you . . ." he stammered hoarsely, "are you by any chance seeking a small boy with no belt?"

"Which way?" shouted the guards. "Which way did he go?"

"That way," said Eric and he nodded toward the sea.

With a clatter of hobnails the two guards were off, Lord Droon sputtering and scolding along behind them.

"No time to shrink down to a boy again," thought Eric. "I'll have to stay a tall man."

On to the castle, Eric raced in his disguise, over fences and thickets, through orchards and fields of corn. Everywhere he saw Patrol Cats, useless and limp, fast asleep on haystacks, dozing in the trees.

Then suddenly, just ahead, he saw the King. He was sitting on a little pile of stones just outside the castle gate. His robe wasn't

pressed; his crown wasn't shined; and he had deep sad circles under both of his eyes.

"Your Majesty . . . Your Majesty!" shouted Eric as he clattered up behind him.

The King paid no attention. Eric leaned down and shouted right into his ear. Very slowly the King turned his head.

"Well," sighed King Birtram, "and who may *you* be?"

"I'm Eric!" cried Eric. He let the robe that was covering him drop to the ground. The King's own red stilts flashed bright in the sun.

Down from the stilts leapt Eric, the page boy. Up onto the stilts sprang Birtram, the King. He drew a great Kingly breath—the first one in weeks. His head shot up high; his chest broadened wide. Birtram of Binn was sturdy, straight and strong again, and every inch a King.

"PATROL CATS!"

It was the loudest command ever shouted in Binn. The King's voice seemed to roll up from deep in his boots. It echoed down the valleys; it rumbled through the hills.

From wherever they had wandered, the cats heard the call. They fell in line; they fell in step; they marched ahead a thousand strong. Up the hill to the Dike Trees they followed Eric and the King.

"Day Cats to the left flank! . . . Night Cats to the right! *Charge!*" the King shouted.

A hundred thousand Nizzards stopped their pecking and sprang to meet the charge. The Dike Trees shook as the cats roared their warcry. The sea's surface swirled into wild raging whirlpools. The noise was heard in Sambaland, five hundred miles away.

The fur flew fast but the feathers flew faster!

It took only ten minutes. The kingdom was saved!

The townsfolk stopped trembling indoors behind their window shades. They rushed out from their houses and filled the air with cheers.

Then the King punished Droon in a most fitting way. He sent him to live by himself, with a guard of Patrol Cats, in that old deserted house with the sign that said "MEASLES." And he made him eat Nizzards three times every day. Stewed Nizzards for breakfast. Cold Nizzards for lunch. Fried Nizzards for supper. And every other Thursday they served him Nizzard hash.

But to Eric, his page boy, the King gave a fine and just reward. He ordered the royal carpenter to make another pair of stilts . . . tall stilts, red and flashing, exactly like his own. From then on, every day at five, they always raced on stilts together.

And when they played they really PLAYED. And when they worked they really WORKED. And the cats kept the Nizzards away from the Dike Trees. And the Dike Trees kept the water back out of the land.

OTHER BOOKS BY DR. SEUSS

AND FOR BEGINNING READERS